Raintree is an imprint of Capstone Global Library Limited, a company
incorporated in England and Wales having its registered office at 264
Banbury Road, Oxford, OX2 7DY – Registered company number: 6695582

www.raintree.co.uk
myorders@raintree.co.uk

Editor: Jill Kalz
Designer: Lori Bye
Pre-media Specialist: Katy LaVigne
Originated by Capstone Global Library Ltd
Printed and bound in India
All illustrations were created digitally.

ISBN: 978 1 4747 9136 6

British Library Cataloguing in Publication Data
A full catalogue record for this book is available from the British Library.

# Harold Hickok Had the Hiccups

by Cassandra Labairon
illustrated by Justin Greathouse

raintree 🍂

a Capstone company — publishers for children

Hillary Hunn hiked in the hills behind her home.
She hummed a happy hmmm-hmmm-hmmm.

One hot day, Hillary Hunn hiked over a field of
hay. She heard HICC-UP! HICC-UP! HICC-UP!

No hog or hound could make that silly sound.

4

Then Hillary saw Harold Hickok high on a hay bale. He said, "HICC-UP! HICC-UP! HICC-UP!"

Harold Hickok had the hiccups.
The hiccups Harold Hickok had.

"Help!" howled Harold. "Help me halt these hiccups, Hillary Hunn!"

"Hold your breath, Harold Hickok," Hillary said. "That should halt the hiccups."

"I tried, Hillary," Harold said. "It didn't help."

"Stand on your head," Hillary said.

Harold tried. But his hiccups didn't halt.

Harold Hickok had the hiccups.
The hiccups Harold Hickok had.

7

"Hop to stop the hiccups, Harold," Hillary said. "Hop, Harold Hickok. Hop like a hare."

Harold hopped in the hay. He hopped like a hare. But the hopping hardly helped.

Harold Hickok had the hiccups.
The hiccups Harold Hickok had.

"What if I howl?" Hillary asked. "Hey, hiccups, hey! Go away! Hey, hiccups, hey! Go away!"

"Hush, Hillary, hush!" Harold said. "HICC-UP! HICC-UP! HICC-UP! My head hurts from your hollering. And I still have the hiccups!"

Hillary Hunn had a hunch. She hid behind some hay. She hoped to scare Harold.

"I hear you, Hillary," Harold Hickok said.
"You're hiding behind the hay! Stop hiding.
Help me halt these hiccups!"

Harold Hickok had the hiccups.
The hiccups Harold Hickok had.

"Have hope, Harold," Hillary said. "I have ideas to help you heal!"

Hillary and Harold hung out with horses. They held out their arms and hovered like hawks. They hoot-hoot-hooted like owls. They how-how-howled like wolves.

"HICC-UP! HICC-UP! HICC-UP!" Harold said. "Hooey! This isn't helping."

Harold Hickok had the hiccups. The hiccups Harold Hickok had.

"Harold," Hillary said, "let's do homework."

"Homework?" Harold said. "I would rather help with housework than do homework. HICC-UP! HICC-UP! HICC-UP!"

"Follow me," Hillary said.

Hillary held Harold's hand as they hurried to her house.

Hillary Hunn and Harold Hickok hung hats on hooks. They hauled clothes from hallway to hamper. They hoovered the whole house.

"Hillary," Harold said, "this housework is hardly helping. HICC-UP! HICC-UP! HICC-UP!"

Harold Hickok had the hiccups.
The hiccups Harold Hickok had.

"Hey!" Hillary said. "Honey heals hiccups! My mum makes pancakes with homemade honey."

Mrs Hunn wanted to help Harold, too. She made heaps of pancakes with homemade honey.

"These hotcakes are heaven!" Harold said without a hiccup.

"Harold, you're healed!" Hillary said.

"Hillary, you're a hero!" Harold cheered. "You helped halt my hiccups! Hooray! Hooray!"

Hillary and Harold hugged. Then they hiked in the hills behind Hillary's home, humming happily.

Harold Hickok had no more hiccups.

23

# More *Tongue Twisters* from Raintree!